# OLIVIA™
## and the Dog Wash

adapted by Natalie Shaw

based on the screenplay "Dog Wash" written by Peggy Sarlin

illustrated by Shane L. Johnson

SIMON SPOTLIGHT
An imprint of Simon & Schuster Children's Publishing Division
New York  London  Toronto  Sydney  New Delhi
1230 Avenue of the Americas, New York, New York 10020
Copyright © 2012 Silver Lining Productions Limited (a Chorion company). All rights reserved. OLIVIA™ and © 2012 Ian Falconer.
All rights reserved. All rights reserved, including the right of reproduction in whole or in part in any form.
SIMON SPOTLIGHT and colophon are registered trademarks of Simon & Schuster, Inc.
For information about special discounts for bulk purchases, please contact Simon & Schuster
Special Sales at 1-866-506-1949 or business@simonandschuster.com.
Manufactured in the United States of America  0312 CWM  First Edition  2 4 6 8 10 9 7 5 3 1
ISBN 978-1-4424-4638-0
ISBN 978-1-4424-4639-7 (eBook)

One day, when they were out in the backyard, Mom told Olivia that she wanted to raise money for the library to buy books for the children's reading room.

"I'll think of some way to help too!" said Olivia. "I'm not sure what, but I'll think of something."

"Can you think and scrub at the same time?" asked Mom. "Perry just jumped in a mud puddle!"

© 2012 SLP. OLIVIA™ and © Ian Falconer

"Hey, Francine!" Olivia called while she washed Perry in the kiddie pool. "Want to help me raise money to buy books for the library?" Before Olivia finished her sentence, Francine was by her side. "If we're talking princess books, I'm in!" Francine said. "What can I do?"

"Hand me that soap, please," said Olivia, "And help me think of something we can do that's really fun."

"Dogs are fun," said Francine, looking at Perry. "But how can we raise money with dogs?"

"Wow, that's it!" Olivia said. "We can have a dog wash!"

Olivia and Francine made fliers for Olivia's Woof-Woof Wash and handed
them out to the neighbors, starting with Firefighter Fred and his Dalmatian.
"Want to come to our dog wash?" asked Francine. "We're raising money for
the library."
 "Well, it is for a good cause," began Firefighter Fred.
"And we guarantee we'll get all his spots out," added Olivia.
"It's a deal," said Firefighter Fred, "but if you don't mind, I'd like to keep the
spots!"

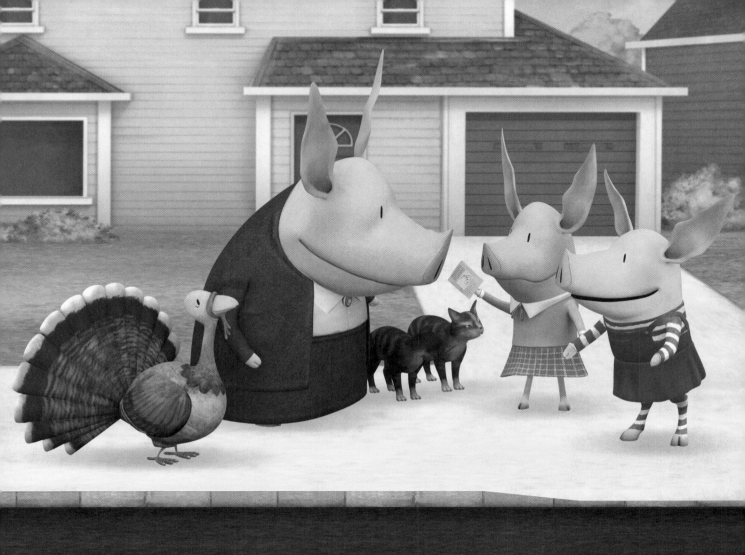

Next Olivia and Francine ran into their teacher, Mrs. Hoggenmuller. "A dog wash to buy books is a wonderful idea!" she said. "But I just have my darling cats and my precious Gobbles. Do you wash turkeys?"

"Sure!" said Olivia. "See you there, Gobbles."

Olivia's friends came by to help wash, rinse, dry, and groom the pets.
"Everybody ready?" asked Olivia. "I'm ready to wash!"
"Ready to suds!" said Ian.

"Ready to rinse!" said Francine.

"Ready to dry," said Julian.

"Ready to groom," said Daisy. She had her assistant pooch, Mrs. Buttercup, by her side.

Then the owners said good-bye to their pets so the washing could begin.

"Be a good doggie," Firefighter Fred said to his Dalmatian.

Everyone was ready to wash the pups—and Gobbles. Perry went first to show the others how it was done.

"Woof, woof! Wet, wet!" said Olivia, when she washed him with water.

"Woof, woof! Suds, suds!" said Ian, as he led Perry through the soap suds.

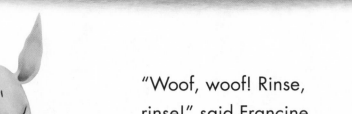

"Woof, woof! Rinse, rinse!" said Francine, as she rinsed him off.

"Woof, woof! Dry . . . um, squirrel!" cried Julian. He was pedaling his drying machine when a squirrel ran past! In an instant all the dogs and one turkey were chasing the squirrel through the backyard.

The dogs were running all over the yard. They were muddier than ever!
It looked like Olivia's Woof-Woof Wash might end up being a washout.
"Now what do we do?" Julian asked. "The dogs are out of control!"

"We just have to find something dogs like more than squirrels," Olivia said.
"I have an idea!"

"A dog bone?" asked Francine.
"Not just any dog bone," replied
Olivia, placing it on Ian's Robo-car.
"A dog bone the dogs can chase!"

"Follow that dog bone!" Olivia shouted,
steering the Robo-car through the dog wash.
The dogs followed the dog bone instead of the squirrel,
and soon Olivia's Woof-Woof Wash was back in business!

When their owners arrived to pick them up, the dogs—and turkey—were sparkling clean. *Woof, woof! Gobble, gobble!* The dogs barked and Gobbles gobbled proudly.

"Is that you, Gobbles?" Mrs. Hoggenmuller asked. "I hardly recognized you!"

"Great job, kids," Mom said. "The library will be able to buy lots of books with the money you raised from your dog wash! Olivia's Woof-Woof Dog Wash was a success!"
Everyone cheered.

That night at bedtime Olivia read one of the books she and Mom bought for the library.

"Just one more page?" Olivia asked, when Mom came to tuck her into bed.

"You can finish it in the morning," Mom said. "You and Perry had a big day."

"Okay. Good night, Mom," Olivia said.

She drifted off to sleep with Perry curled up next to her, smelling nice and clean.